TAKE MY HUSBAND, PLEASE!!!

Written By: Leilani Starr

TAKE
MY
HUSBAND
PLEASE!!!

Dedicated To Kayleigh Blaze
You Truly Amaze

Table of Contents

Chapter One
High School Friends

Lisa and Mary were the new girls.   Both of them had

moved around the same, a lot.   Lisa's parents had

always been travelers.   Even after Lisa and her

sister Krystal were born.   It seems they never found

just the right place to stay.   They would move to a new

place, usually for a job.   Lisa's dad was a jack

of all trades, master of none.   He would get bored of

the everyday routine and would constantly look for new

opportunities.

Unfortunately for the family it meant moving around a

lot.   Lisa never enjoyed the gypsy lifestyle.

Whenever they did move they would sell or get rid of

almost everything and take just a few days worth of

clothes and personal things.   When they got to the

new place they would find new things.   Most of the

time they were donated or thrift store finds.   Lisa

always felt she should have brand new things.   She

did not want other people's discarded items.

Lisa's mother would always tell her that it did not matter

about material possessions.   It was about family being

together.   For Lisa this was not something she was

comforted by.   She wanted new things.   She wanted

only one house.   She wanted new clothes.   She

was tired of having only used items.

Lisa had always lived with her mother and father.

Mary had only ever known a mother that always had

priorities above Mary.   Mary had grown up with her

grandparents.   Her mother was in and out of her life.

The only time Mary's mother was around was when

there was money to be made if you had a kid.

The few times Mary did live with her mother her time

was spent trying to keep her mother from using drugs

or drinking alcohol. The one thing Mary's mother did love was to party, and party she did every chance she got. Which would mean Mary was left alone or worse left with someone her mother had just met.

On the few occasions she would take Mary to her grandparent's house, most times they would refuse to give her back. They would keep Mary until her mom would clean up or prove she was taking care of Mary. Of course, as Mary grew older she would talk about the things that would happen at her mother's house and she knew that she was afraid when she lived at her mother's house.

Mary just never knew who would be at her house on a daily basis and most of the time they were passed out. Sometimes in chairs, sometimes on the floor and sometimes even in her own bed.

When she lived with her grandparent's things were less

chaotic.   They worked very hard to give Mary
everything she needed to live a normal, routine daily
life.   As much as Mary liked the comfort of her
grandparent's house, she missed her mom and just
wished her mom would stay home and not party so
much with everyone.

As much as Mary wanted that to happen it just never
did and probably never would.   Even as Mary got
older she and her mother were more like sisters or
friends than mother and daughter.   All Mary ever
wanted was a mother who took care of her.   Her
grandparents did their best but they were tired, old and
they were getting sick.   They too wished their
daughter would stop partying and provide a proper
home for her daughter.

Now Lisa and Mary would be attending the same
school in the fall.   As soon as they met they were

instant friends.   New schools were always difficult for both of them and now they felt like they would at least have each other.   Even though their pasts were different they were both looking for a better future, that they were sure of.   They knew they were on the same page about that.

Lisa's family had moved to the small town for a fresh start.   Lisa's dad did a lot of side jobs and was looking to continue that, while her mom looked for a job too. Rents were cheaper and Lisa and her sister, Krystal were getting older and looking forward to staying in the same school for a while.   They didn't know if it would happen but they hoped it would.   Lisa's mom hoped it would last for a while too.

Mary had been left with her grandparents yet again. There was always some trip, friends or place that needed her mom in attendance.   Mary's grandparents, Joe and Dottie were always there for Mary. As she got older it became more and more important to have a good example for her to follow. As Mary got older it was cool to party and her mother not only encouraged it but provided opportunities for her to party with all kinds of people. Mary always found herself surrounded by partying people. After awhile it becomes easier to join in than be bothered by the partiers.

Mary did want to have friends but most of them just wanted to party with her mother or her mother's friends instead of hanging out with Mary.

Mary's mother was always the life of the party. Always getting carried away with jokes and nicknames which were difficult for Mary to keep up with. So many of the kids did not have any opportunity to party with their parents and Mary's mother would beg her to go out with her.   Having Mary around was just a good conversation piece for her mother to talk about with anyone who was willing to listen to her.   Most people thought they were sisters.   Many times this left Mary in an uncomfortable position.   Her mother did not have to go to school every day and see them.   It was difficult for Mary to handle.

Mary's grandparent's house was always a good move away from that life.   Her grandparents insisted Mary be given a less chaotic lifestyle, even if that meant they had to provide it.   Mary was in high school now and she was choosing to spend more time with her mom.   That was something her grandparents were not happy about.   Mary was growing up and looking to fit in.   This was one way her grandparents did not want her to choose.   They tried hard to keep Mary focused on school and being lady-like.   Mary liked to dress up but she liked to relax too.

Her mother was the opposite of her grandparents, but for Mary she always wanted something more in the middle. Her grandparents were strict to start with but after raising their daughter and seeing the choices she was making it pushed them to be even more strict with Mary. This created a rebellious attitude towards not only her grandparents but towards her mom as well.

Her mother would always party, instead of everything. She had no desire to be responsible or tied down to anything. If you tried to pin her down she would run for sure. Mary just wanted a mom who would be around for her and her mother didn't even want to try. Mary's mom knew her parents would provide Mary with the things she needed in life. So she believed that made it okay for her to leave the responsibility of raising Mary to her parents. Mary loved her grandparents but she just wanted her mom to do mom

things and her mom was just not interested.

Chapter Two
Meeting The One

Lisa and Mary met in the summer, while working in a

youth employment program. As soon as they met they

knew they would be friends, especially when they

would be going to the same school.   Lisa and Mary

both had lots of friends at their old schools and usually

did not have much trouble making new friends.

They had both moved a lot and now both had been told

they would be living there for a while.

Lisa and Mary liked hanging out at the park.   It was

pretty much the only place people could meet and

hang out.   There was a larger town with a theatre and

bowling alley about forty miles away.   It was few and

far between the times they would drive the forty miles.

So hanging out at the park was the best

thing to do.

There was a pool for the summer and big fields with

baseball diamonds and playground areas for the kids

to play. Most of the older kids would hang out

around the horse shoe pits.

The high school class for that year was about 200 kids.

Even kids that were old enough to drive and had cars

did not travel the forty miles a lot. The winding roads

were dangerous and many accidents over the years

had resulted in many stories of crazy things that had

happened, especially in the winter months. School

would be starting soon and Lisa and Mary were busy

meeting friends and enjoying their new experiences.

Lisa and Mary had personalities that were similar and

both were looking to rise above the situations they

lived in and be more stable. They wanted to

have the money they need to get what they want.

Both Lisa and Mary wanted to get married and have

families. They knew things would be different for them and they would be nothing like their parents.

Both Lisa and Mary got new school clothes for the new school year. Lisa was so happy they did not have to shop at the thrift store this year, or have only hand me downs from relatives or friends. Her dad found work right away and things were good for now. Her mom seemed happy and it looked like things were changing.

The high school was decent size for the small amount of students and they even had an alternative high school at the other end of town for those students that needed an optional school plan to accommodate their life.

Lisa and Mary were picking classes and looking forward to meeting new friends. Lisa's sister Krystal was often with Mary and Lisa. Krystal was about 10 months older than Lisa and their family had moved around a lot so the sisters had spent a lot of time together and often times had a lot of the same friends. This year was going to be different. Lisa and Mary both knew their lives were changing.

School started and Lisa and Mary worked in to a routine. Filling their days with classes and friends working hard to keep up their grades. As well as spending time with friends, meeting new friends and trying new things.

With the new school year came a trend of having a party at the house of the parents who were out of town. Most often it was one family but sometimes there were several houses to choose from as parents felt the need for a weekend getaway. Leaving their house with their "responsible teenager." Even a responsible teenager can have a weak moment and things can get out of control faster than you can imagine. Many a parent came home to "a funny thing happened while you were away."

Lisa's house was never an option.   Even if her parents did go out of town she would never have her friends over.   Mary's house would never work either. Her grandparents never went away for the weekend and if they did they would find someone for Mary to stay with while they were gone.   Both Lisa and Mary would follow the parties at other people's house and it was getting to be what they all wanted to do on the weekends.   It was different every weekend and a great way to meet guys.   That is where Lisa met Mark and Mary met Jack.

Lisa's sister Krystal also met a guy named Mike. They seemed to get along well.   They spent a lot of time together and before anyone realized what was happening Krystal was pregnant.   Krystal

and Mike were both in the same grade and they both

knew they wanted to finish school and graduate early,

before their baby was born.   Mike's family had a

remodeling business and he had always worked

there during the summers and to help out during busy

times.   He would work there full time when he did

graduate.

Krystal was having a boy. They decided they would

name him David.   Krystal was happy that she had

found a great guy and now they would have a baby

together.

Lisa missed spending time with Krystal but she knew

Krystal would do whatever she needed to do and they

were both growing up now and they would probably be

spending less time together.   They did make a point of

getting together every few days just to keep up with

what was going on with each other.   Lisa knew Krystal

would be okay and it did seem like Mike really

cared for her.

Mike was really good for Krystal.   He really seemed to

love her.   While he did have clear ideas of what he

wanted he did seem to want Krystal to have those

same ideas too.   While Krystal did share a lot of those

ideas she too was a bit of a free-spirit and did not

always find herself locked down to one idea.

Krystal always liked to try new things and sometimes

that did not make Mike too happy.   They both seemed

willing to give it a chance and try to make it work.

Lisa and Krystal's relationship was different now.

Besides the fact that Krystal was tired a lot.   She was

busy with Mike and getting things ready for their new

baby.   They were both looking forward to having a

baby.   Krystal and Mike were willing to work out the

life that was set in front of them and raise their son together. Their parents were disappointed that this was the way things were turning out but they were all happy that Krystal and Mike had decided to make the best of things together. That would be the best for all of them, as long as it worked out.

Lisa and Mary were happy for Krystal but could not imagine having a baby at their age. They knew they would have kids one day but they were certainly not thinking about that now or anytime soon. They too were working towards building a strong relationship with their new boyfriends. They knew lots of things would be changing in their lives now and they were excited about it.

Jack and Mark could not be more different. They had opposite personalities and ways of thinking. They put up with each other for Mary And Lisa. The four of them did not spend a lot of time all together so it was not a big deal. They would either be together as couples or would be in a bigger group. This did not stop Mary and Lisa from hanging out together. They found common ground with each other. They just got along and really enjoyed being friends and spending time together. They had hoped Jack and Mark would be better friends but that didn't happen and they knew it probably never would.

Lisa and Mary would spend as much time together as they could. They did have several classes together and both rode the bus to and from school. They would also get together after school most weekdays and on the weekends. They would all be together with their friends as much as they could. They knew their time would not last forever so they wanted to make sure they made the best of it. They always had fun together.

Krystal was busy and tired a lot. Most times it would

be just Lisa and Mary. Any time spent with new

boyfriends was closely monitored and limited. They

both got distracted quickly and limiting the time spent

with boyfriends worked out well for now. Lisa and

Mary were at least able to spend time together.

They often spent time talking about how things would

be for them in the future and what they would do. Lisa

and Mary both had big dreams of how they thought

their lives would turnout.

They just knew they would have all the things they

wanted and more. They were sure everything would

go according to their plan. All they needed to do was

keep working towards their goals. One thing that was

clear to all of them is they would need to graduate high

school.

Lisa and Mary knew they wanted to work full-time.

They wanted to have money that they made on their own. As much as the plan was to have good husbands who would take good care of them, they both knew they wanted the opportunity to work and make their own money. They both had too many plans to sit back and wait to be taken care of. Even though both Mary and Lisa believed Jack and Mark would give them everything they ever wanted.

As much as Jack and Mark wanted to spend time with Mary and Lisa they did enjoy the time they were not allowed to be together. Both Jack and Mark would help their families a lot. Jack's dad always needed things done around the house and Mark's parents always had things they wanted Mark to do for them.

Krystal was due to have her baby in the Spring. She was doing well in her pregnancy, no real complications. She was just really tired and after school spent most of her time resting and reading books about pregnancy and having a baby. While Krystal was surprised to find out she was pregnant she was taking it seriously and was trying to do everything she could to prepare. Mike was working a lot at the family business, while supporting Krystal through all the changes going on. They were both attending the alternate high school to work through their high school requirements at a quicker pace than regular high school. They were hoping to complete high school by the time David was born but it would be close. They would both most likely have to go back for a short time after he was born. They knew they wanted their diplomas so they would do what they needed to do. It just did not seem there was enough hours in the day to do everything they needed to do before the baby was born. They were both still working hard to get what they could done.

Krystal missed hanging out with her friends but she knew she needed to do everything she could to raise their baby.   She wanted David to have everything he needed growing up and she wanted to make sure she did everything she could to make it happen.

Krystal also was not happy with the way she grew up. She loved her parents but always wanted the security her parents were not interested in providing.   Krystal wanted to know where she would be living, sleeping or working and was not interested in always looking for a better place.   Krystal knew if she wanted these things she would have to work hard for them.   She knew they would not be handed to her without working for it.   Krystal was ready to do what it took to make the best life she could and to have a stable environment to raise her son with Mike.   Krystal was happy that it seemed they were both interested in providing for their child.

Even if that meant she would not be able to hang out with her friends or Lisa as much or even at all for a while.

Lisa was happy for Krystal but missed hanging out with her. She hoped they would be able to hang out again soon. Lisa and Krystal used to always be together but now it was different and there were new things and changes happening all around. They were all excited about the changes and were working into their new routines and daily life.

Prom would be coming up soon and the girls would all be looking for dresses. It was always the highlight of spring. Even if you didn't get ask to the prom everyone would go. It was one of the few things they did do every year. Every class looked forward to it. There was always a lot of planning that went into this big celebration every year. They would all be going.

Even Krystal and Mike would be going. Any of the events or big programs the high school and alternate high school would celebrate together. This gave all the students the ability to see that graduation was possible for everyone. No matter what your circumstances are. It worked out well because even though some kids went to the alternate high school they started at the high school and all the kids knew each other.

Both schools would have their own anyway, combining them would just create a bigger program for everyone. Lisa and Mary went all out for their dresses. Mark and Jack were seniors this year. They knew they wanted to look good at the prom. Lisa had no problem convincing Mark to go and the only reason Jack was going is because Mary said she was going whether Jack did or not. Everyone looked forward to prom. People could not imagine what it would be like not to go because everyone would always go, even Jack.

Krystal found a great dress for herself. She looked great and it was nice for Krystal and Mark to be able to relax and spend the evening with their friends and be able to step away, even for a night, from their grown up changes happening so quickly. They all had fun. There was so much to do. Most of the town showed up for the prom. It was always nice to see so many come together and enjoy their time without major problems and drama. It seemed like everyone always enjoyed themselves. There was no reason to cause trouble or not show up.

While Krystal and Mike were settling in to their grown up responsibilities. Krystal seemed to get bored quickly with all the new responsibilities. Not that she wasn't happy about all of it. she thought it was pretty cool that she had stepped in to such an easy transition.

All she had to do was go along with things. While that was an easy task, Krystal soon grew very bored with not a lot to fill her time. She would hang out with her friends and for Krystal that meant trouble.

Krystal would always lose sight of the bigger picture. Krystal was a free spirit and would often get caught up in the moment and not worry so much about the long term. While Krystal was out with her friends they were all partying and having fun. When Krystal got home Mike was waiting with a drug test. Krystal tested positive and Mike took the results to the police department. Krystal was in a battle for her freedom and her baby. While Mike was tired of Krystal's outings, he knew this would be the way to get the upper hand as far as control of the baby when he was born. Krystal could not believe Mike would be so sneaky and take their personal business to the police.

Krystal grew up afraid of the police and now they were
investigating her with the help of Mike, her own
husband.   Krystal would do whatever she needed
to do to keep her baby.   She knew it was because she
had been around the partying and she really did not
have a problem.   She was just out having fun with her
friends and had no idea Mike would be trying to drug
test her.

After a court hearing, Krystal was required to submit to
random drug testing for the next year.   If she remained
clean she would not have a problem, they would no
longer monitor her.   Krystal knew it would be easy for
her to do that because her and Mike had both partied
before but Mike didn't like that Krystal would go out
with her friends.   While Mike knew that Krystal only
participated occasionally.   It was not something she
did every time they went out.   He was just able to
document her use through the courts and if she said

something about him it would look like she was just trying to direct attention away from herself.

When Krystal went into labor the social worker was with them so that the baby, David, could be tested right away. Krystal had quit partying all together after the court proceedings. She knew they would not deny her access to her son. After Mike took her to court Krystal was having a difficult time being with him. She was so angry that he would do something like that to her . He knew she would be a good mom and that she did not have a problem. The only reason he did it was for control. Mike just wanted to make sure he was not shut out of David's life. This is just the only way he knew how to make that happen. He was able to do it quickly and with not much resistance but once it was done there was no going back.

Everything went well for Krystal, David and Mike during

delivery.   Krystal and Mike were getting along and David was healthy and was quick to deliver, with no complications.   After a short stay in the hospital Krystal and David went home to be with Mike and to continue their life together with their new baby. This was easier said than done for both Krystal and Mike.   Neither of them trusted each other anymore. And while they both loved David,   they agreed they would be better off living separately.   With the trust gone for both of them all they did was fight when they were together.   While they both loved their time with David they knew they would have to split their time. Both Krystal and Mike appreciated the relationship David had with each of them and knew that would be important for David to always have that with both of them.

They both knew the importance of both mother and father in their child's life and they were both willing to do what it took to provide that for their son.

They created a fifty/fifty custody plan.   Split right

down the middle, time, expenses and everything.

They may have quickly decided they do not belong

together but both wanted to allow time for the other

parent as well as value their own time.   With

summertime right around the corner Krystal and Lisa

would have time to hang out together.   Lisa would be

working in the summer but Krystal moved back in with

their parents after she split from Mike.   With Krystal

now back at their parent's house they would be able to

spend more time together.   It would only be for a while

until Krystal could find a job and save up some money.

Krystal knew she needed to get a job but she was

trying so hard to be a good mom there was not a lot of

time to work even with splitting the time with Mike.

There was a lot to do to take care of a baby and Krystal

and Mike were both very lucky they had each other.

Krystal knew it would be more difficult to live separately when they chose it but she knew it was better than the alternative, living together.

Krystal knew soon enough she would be working and have her own place. Mike really wanted Krystal to be home for David so they agreed he would help Krystal during the first years of David's life so she could stay home with him.

Krystal was able to get her own place and not worry about working for now. Krystal was grateful Mike was willing to provide for their son. Krystal knew she would be working soon enough but at least for now she could be there full time for her son.

David was a good baby but even good babies are a lot of work. Even between the two of them it was a lot of work. As David grew both Krystal and Mike worked to be big parts of David's life. That even meant being

37

together at times to be with David.   That was one thing

they were both committed to.   Raising the best kid

they could regardless of the things that had gone on

between them.

While Lisa and Mary spent time with Krystal neither

one of them could imagine having a baby to take care

of at their age.   Mark and Jack were not friends but

they knew of each other.   Mark spent most of his time

around the jocks at school while Jack spent time with

the hunters or survivalists in school.   Not that Jack

was a survivalist at all.   He just enjoyed weapons and

the hunt.   Jack definitely had a dark side which Mary

saw as mysterious and that made her curious.

While Mark did not actually play sports he did hang out

with all the jocks.   He watched a lot of sports and did

play sports for fun but not for any organized teams.

He liked to play but not for a league.   He wanted to

use his head to make money not his body.   His

father was a firefighter and he always knew he would

be a firefighter like his father.   His mother was so

proud of his desire to be a firefighter.   She

had told people all of his life that he would be a

firefighter.   Mark knew there was no question.   His

future would be as a firefighter.   Lisa was excited to

meet a guy who had goals of a career not just the next

job.   Mark liked Lisa a lot.   They seemed to have

quite a bit in common and they were having fun getting

to know each other.

Lisa and Mark would sit and talk for hours.   Mark liked

to talk about his plans and Lisa loved to listen.   Lisa

just knew Mark was the one for her.   He had

a plan and wanted to be something and a firefighter at

that.   Someone who would save the day.   They would

be married and have kids.   She wanted that more than

anything and Mark was that guy she just knew it.

Mary and Jack talked but mostly Mary talked. While they both drank a lot. Mary loved the thought of what her and Jack could be. The problem was Jack was only in it for the admiration Mary would give him, all the time. Whenever she waivered at all Jack would get angry and Mary would immediately return to gushing about how great Jack was and how everything would be okay. Jack didn't have much to say. For the most part he would just watch Mary go back and forth trying to build this relationship. He seemed to just be along for the ride but he did have his ideas about how his girlfriend should look, act and respond. If she did not he was sure to remind her every time. Mary didn't mind. She knew it would all work out and that Jack was the man of her dreams. He just needed some work.

Chapter Three
Starting Out

Mary's grandparents, Joe and Dottie were not happy with her choices in boyfriends.   In fact they told her that she should focus on her career and her future, not spending time trying to build up another person. Especially one who was just looking to manipulate and control Mary.   Jack was worried about himself, today, he was not looking to live happily ever after. He was just living and Mary wanted to help Jack see they could live happily ever after.   Mary would stop at nothing to show Jack that they could be happy together.

Lisa's parents were thrilled with Mark. They pushed Lisa to be with him as much as she could.   Lisa's parents did not expect Lisa to have any career.   They believed she would finish high school, get married, have a family and that would be that.   Lisa's parents

had no desire to own a big house, car or luxurious

things.   They lived simply and liked it.   So knowing

Lisa wanted expensive things in her life they knew the

only way she would have those things would be if she

found someone who could give her those things.

Mark seemed to want these things too.   So it

appeared to be a good match for both of them.   Even

though her parents thought she needed someone to

give her all these things Lisa believed she could

work and provide all these things she wanted for

herself.   She wanted Mark in her life but she wanted a

career as well.

With Mark looking to be a firefighter it would be

seasonal at first and Lisa would have to work for

awhile.   That was in the future and right now Lisa and

Mark were enjoying getting to know each other. School

was tough for Lisa, her focus was on Mark and their

future together.   Mary wanted to keep up with her studies.   She was an excellent student and did not have much trouble keeping up with her class.   Her troubles came when she would always sneak away to spend time with Jack.

Jack would constantly tell her that he would take care of her and she did not need to worry about working. Jack always wanted a girlfriend who would stay home and cater to his every need.   He did not see the point of Mary spending so much time keeping up with school work when she could spend that time keeping him happy.   Whatever that would be at the time. Jack was cold and calculating and spent a lot of time telling Mary what she should do and how she should do it.   This was the big reason her grandparents did not want her to spend time with Jack.

With Mary sneaking out to see Jack she was obviously

not talking to them about her concerns with her relationship with Jack. Jack was not an easy going person.

He had explosive anger episodes which came on quickly and would subside but not until fear and aggression would grow and then calm, regret and forgiveness would overcome him.

Mary was sure with her at Jack's side she could curb his anger and aggression and he would be the best thing that ever happened to her. Mary honestly believed that with work it could happen and everything would fall into place.

Lisa and Mary both knew they needed to graduate high school. While Mary was a good student Jack took a lot of Mary's time and she struggled to keep her grades up. Lisa struggled in school but always pretended it was just a game. Lisa knew she needed to graduate and she wanted to graduate and she would do whatever she had to do to make it happen.

Mark was busy working through his own studies but he had his plans laid out and knew how he would make things happen the way he wanted. Lisa tried to model her choices around Mark's choices. This worked for a couple of reasons. One, she knew she had a good plan and two, they would be able to spend more time together.

Jack did not really care at all for school. He was just putting in his time until it was over. That made it even more difficult for Mary to keep up with school. Her grandparents were strong and strict when it came to education. They didn't necessarily think Mary would go to college but they did know she would graduate high school.

Mary knew they were right about pushing her to keep

up with school but it was a lot of work keeping Jack happy and he was so quick to lose his temper. Mary was always up for a challenge and between Jack, school and her grandparents she certainly had them.

Jack and Mark did not necessarily get along at all but they did all hang out in the same group of friends so they did spend a lot of time around each other. They didn't really like or dislike each other but it was clear that if Lisa and Mary were not friends they would not talk.   The only reason they did talk was because Mary and Lisa were friends.

Mark and Jack did have one thing in common.   They were both one year ahead of Lisa and Mary.   They would graduate the year before Mary and Lisa would. This did cause conflict occasionally but for the most part it gave Jack and Mark a little bit of an edge as they would get out first but it also could work against them

as couples based on what they do with that year. Lisa

was sure her and Mark would be together forever.

Mary knew she could "fix" Jack and he would be the

best partner ever. Even if it didn't last forever it was a

project that Mary set her sights on and would stop at

nothing to make it happen. She always tried to keep

Jack happy at all costs.

This created less explosions and resulting fallout from

his aggressive physical attacks. Jack was not a

friendly guy and spent a lot of time calling people out to

start fights. Mary could not always stop that behavior

so she just tried to keep her distance when he

exploded at others. That way it would not backfire

and be turned towards her. As much as Mary

wanted to be with Jack she had witnessed firsthand

Jack's violence and altered sense of reality he created

in his own mind. Jack could easily turn something he

had done into someone else's fault in no time flat. A

lot of time he would explode on Mary and she would be the one apologizing for whatever had made him angry.

Mary really believed in Jack and thought that so many people were "out to get him" and she needed to "be in his corner" to let him know they were going to be together forever.

Lisa did not have to worry so much about Mark. Mark spent most of his time pleasing others. It wasn't always about him. It was about what others wanted for him. His mother was a strong influence in his life. She custom built his future for him. Now all he had to do was carry it out.

Lisa tried hard to get along with Mark's mother but she made it clear from the start that Lisa was not good enough for her son. She had pictured a beautiful girl from a wonderful family who adored her son. While

Lisa was pretty and did adore Mark, she was not from a "good family", according to Mark's mother. This left Lisa struggling to live up to the expectations Mark's mother placed on her. As much as Mark wanted to please his mother, Lisa was just one thing they did not agree on. Mark and his mother would argue constantly about the time he spent with Lisa. They challenged each other with obstacles to show the pitfalls and achievements in their lives.

High school was quickly coming to an end for all of them. Mark and Jack would graduate soon and Lisa and Mary were scheduled to work the summer between their junior and senior year to make money and gain work experience.

While Mark was working toward being hired for the season as a firefighter. This would start his path to being hired full time. It was always a seasonal start when working as a firefighter. As soon as Mark graduated he would work the first fire season. As much as he argued with his mom about Lisa he was still on the path to be a firefighter.

Jack and Mary were planning to save all their money and move to the city. While Jack did not have things planned out as much, he was definitely going to find work and save money. He found Mary who wanted to move with him. Jack knew he had always wanted out of the small town. They figured they would save all year and Mary would work the summers and they would have money to get themselves a place to live and keep them going until they found jobs. Mary had never wanted to move away before but now that Jack wanted to move Mary was ready to go. Mary thought if they moved to the city Jack would want to be a couple and a family and everything would be wonderful.

It seemed Mary and Lisa had found partners and they were planning their futures. While they would no longer live in the small town together they would surely keep in touch and maybe they would visit each other. While Lisa was curious about the city, Mark had no desire to go anywhere away from the small town. He knew he would stay close his whole life.

Lisa was okay with that because she felt Mark was security and it would be okay as long as she followed his plan. She knew it was what she wanted and Mark would be her partner along the way.

Chapter Four
Baby Makes Three

Mary and Jack were quickly making plans for the move.   With Jack graduating their time was coming near.   They kept quiet about their plans to avoid arguments about moving.   Mary's grandparents were hopeful she would not move away, especially with Jack.   They saw Jack as someone who de-railed Mary's best efforts.

With Jack around she spent most of her time trying to keep Jack happy.   This was a difficult task because Jack enjoyed seeing Mary always spending so much energy on him.   Mary just chose not to talk a lot about Jack with her grandparents.   They knew she was spending time with him and his control over her was becoming very clear.

All they had was the little time they had left with Mary in

high school.   After that Mary would be eighteen and

would be making her own decisions.   At least

for now Mary was keeping her grades up and seemed

to be focused on graduating high school.

Mary and Lisa were working for the County during the

summer. They did both enjoy making their own money.

It gave them a feeling of being in control.   Even if it

was just for a little while until they spent their money or

put it into savings for the future move and life together.

Lisa's older sister Krystal would have graduated the

same year as Mark and Jack.   Lisa knew after she

graduated her parents would probably be off to travel

again.   She just hoped they waited until she did

graduate.   If they were to pack up now it would surely

devastate her world.

Lisa knew she would not want to leave this small town

ever because that would mean she would not see Mark

again.   Her parents had not really said anything but they never did.   She hoped that would continue.   There was no way to know how long it would last. Lisa just hoped her parents knew how important it was to her.   She only had a little more than a year left and it just seemed it was all working out as planned, as far as Lisa was concerned.

Lisa and Mary would work the summer at the same office.   Mark would work his first fire season and Jack would be working with a fencing company as soon as he graduated.   It was hard work but it paid well and Jack knew he would need to save as much money as possible for the move.   Rents were higher and they did not know anyone in the city.   In the small town everyone knows everyone and it was easy to find work and get hired.   The city would be tougher but Jack was no stranger to hard work.   He would do whatever it takes to keep good money coming in.

Everything was coming together as planned. It was now just a matter of time. Mark had always helped out at the fire station. His family had a history of firefighters. Mark's father and his uncle were firefighters and his grandfather was a firefighter too.

Being from the small town most of the families were volunteer firefighters. Mark knew how shifts worked and what happened on the shift. The firehouse he would be working at worked four days on duty and three days off. Mark knew how shifts worked and knew he would have no problems keeping up. He worked hard and enjoyed the work.

Mark was also very athletic and would always push through until the job was done. Lisa knew how much working as a firefighter meant to Mark. This was one common ground Lisa and Mark's mother had. Lisa always tried to make the most of it but Mark's mom was convinced Lisa would not be around for long so she wanted nothing to do with her. Even though Mark's mom made it perfectly clear where their relationship stood. Lisa continued to try to break the ice with her. She would always try to bring up conversations with Mark's mom that they had common ground on. It was difficult, as Mark's mother would continue to either ignore Lisa or remind her of another matter that they were not in agreement on . Lisa just knew she was not going anywhere and she would break through to Mark's mom sooner or later.

Mark was not happy that Lisa and his mother did not get along but he really cared for Lisa and thought if his mother would just get to know her and give her a chance. It just seemed his mother would not give Lisa any break because her family was not wealthy or well established. She told Mark on a regular basis he deserved a girl of better quality and upbringing. Mark just told Lisa to keep trying.   He hoped his mother would come around.

Lisa's parents always wanted Lisa to bring Mark around but she would not.   She was afraid her parents would say something that would make her look bad.   She just always told Mark and his family they were busy.

Jack's family was never present.   Even Jack didn't want to be around them much.   He would see them as little as possible but he would usually go alone and would not stay long.   Jack's dad would be alone in the house when Jack left.   His mother had taken off a long time ago and she did not look back.   Jack's brother, Bill had moved out when he turned eighteen and never looked back.   He called occasionally but would not lift a finger to help his dad and Jack felt the same way.

Jack's dad was better off alone anyway.   Then he

would have no one to bully in to doing all the daily chores. He would have to do them himself or pay someone to do them. Either way neither one of his sons wanted anything to do with him.

Jack's brother Bill always tried to pass the blame to Jack. Always saying Jack was younger and still living in the house so he would have to stay with their father. Jack knew that was not going to happen and no one was going to make him stay. He was leaving and that was for sure.

His dad knew Jack was leaving as soon as he could but he also knew he could not leave until he was eighteen. As little family unity as there appeared to be in Jack's family he knew he had to stay until he was eighteen or his dad would cause nothing but trouble. He just knew as soon as he was eighteen there would be nothing his father could do.

Mary was ready to go as soon as they could but her grandparents would have none of her talk of leaving before she was eighteen either.   This would mean Jack would have to hang around for an entire year before they could move to the city.   Mary knew she would have to keep Jack happy so he would wait for her and they could move to the city together.   Mary would help Jack with whatever he needed that helped him keep his overall anger level down.   This would keep Mary from fighting with Jack.   Even with all her hard work Jack would have fits of rage which would last for hours and sometimes days.   Even with all this Mary just knew Jack was the one she wanted to marry and be with.

The best part about Jack was that he was a good hard worker.   He was always on time and ready to work. This came from years of working with his dad and trying to live up to his dad's expectations.   This is all

Jack knew when work was involved. Be on time and finish the job. Jack found work doing construction. He worked hard and made himself available for any shifts they could use him to work. Jack was good with his money too. While he did go out and buy some things, he was not out to overspend. He knew he would have to put money away if he wanted to move and he knew he did want to move. He knew there was more out there in the world than this small town had to offer for him.

Mary enjoyed working too and she knew Jack would want her to work for now. Once she got herself established with a job she knew Jack would be okay with her continuing to work. Even though Jack had a problem with Mary being around other people.

According to Jack she was always sleeping with all the

guys and planning with the girls to leave him and live on her own. Mary just knew that Jack would change his ways and not be so aggressive and controlling. She knew that everything would be okay. Jack was like her project. She felt with time Jack would be the man she had always wanted as a husband. She just knew he would be a great dad and they would be a happy family. Jack was annoyed by Mary's nagging but she did really seem to care about him and that made him happy.

Lisa knew Mark would be a good husband. His mother had made sure to instill the values of a good provider in him from early on. Mark would talk all the time about getting married and moving in to a house together, having babies and living happily ever after. While Lisa was always interested in listening to Mark, sometimes she felt he did not believe she could live up to her side of their relationship and he would constantly remind her of her short comings.   While

Lisa would get upset at his delivery sometimes she

would take his suggestions to heart.   She knew her

parents had not given her as much guidance as other

parents gave their children and Lisa wanted the picture

Mark would paint of their future.   She felt that if she

continued to learn and work on new skills she could

make it happen.   Lisa always wanted the experience

of that stable family.   One that lived in the same town

for most of their lives.   Mark was the third generation

of his family growing up not only in the same town but

in the same house on the same piece of property.

Lisa's friends always thought she had the cool parents

but Lisa hated the fact that her parents interacted with

her friends as if they were their own friends.

More than once her friends would come to the house

and end up spending more time talking with her

parents than to her.   Lisa always wished her parents

were not the free spirits they would always prove to be. Lisa just felt cheated in the parents department. She felt like she got parents who wanted to be her friends not her parents. She did not have parents who wanted to push their kids to achieve their goals and push them until they achieved them. Lisa's parents only advice was always, "do what makes you happy."

While this advice was nice to hear, it was always the same. Never even offering their opinion. Only saying "you are free to choose what you want", not what they thought would be best. Lisa always felt they never took her seriously but that was their attitude about everything. That was however, until it came to Mark. Lisa's parents felt he was bossing her around and forcing her to do things she would not have done before.

Lisa wanted to do everything right. She would do

whatever she could to make Mark happy. She felt that

Mark knew what he was talking about to get what

they both wanted. The happily ever after. The white

picket fence, the whole thing.

Lisa and Mary would be starting their senior year soon.

Mark was busy working at the fire house and enjoying

every minute of it. Jack and his father had come to an

agreement that Jack would stay while Mary was in her

last year of high school and they would leave after she

graduated. Jack's dad was not looking forward to the

day he would leave but would not let on that it bothered

him at all. He would remind Jack all the time that he

would be leaving soon and it did not really matter what

he thought.

They all knew their senior year would go quickly.

They would be getting all of their credits and future

plans in order. Both Lisa and Mary were on target to

graduate.   They had worked hard to keep up and now would graduate at the same time.   While Mary and Jack talked about moving away Lisa knew it was not happening right now and they had time to enjoy their last year together.

Lisa and Mary would get together to practice cooking and looking through magazines to pick out things they wanted in their houses or for their weddings.   They knew they wanted it all.   They would talk for hours about how things were going to be.

Lisa and Mark would go out to eat and to see movies together.   They spent a lot of time talking about their future too.   Mark was enjoying his time at the fire house.   He knew this was definitely the job for him. Lisa missed Mark when he was working but she knew this was what they both wanted.   She knew when Mark did get hired full time they would have their dream come true.

Mary and Jack would go out to eat as well but they spent most of their time working. They were both working as much as they could so they would have enough money to move. They wanted to make sure they would not have to come back to the small town for any reason. They just wanted to be as far away from the small town as they could get.

Lisa and Mary's senior year would soon be coming to an end. Lisa planned that her and Mark would get married in the fall and move in together and have babies. Mark, however, was not so sure he wanted to get married right away. He knew he wanted to wait until he was hired on full time. Lisa knew that getting hired full time could take three to five years. Mark had already been working for almost one year. Three to five years seemed like forever to Lisa and she just wanted to get married now.

Mark always tried to remind her if they waited Lisa would more likely get the big wedding she wanted but right now it would have to be a small wedding because that would be all they could afford for now.

Lisa hated that he was right but she knew that he probably was right and she should wait. Lisa however, did not have a lot of patience and was always afraid Mark's mother would convince him he would be better off with another choice of a partner.

Mary and Jack planned to get married the summer before they left. That way they would be husband and wife and less people would question their choice to move to the city. While they knew this is what they wanted, they also knew not everyone would be happy with their decision. Mary knew her grandparents did not want to move again. They were tired and just wanted to relax and enjoy themselves. This small town was the best place for that. They had a nice little house, not a lot of grounds to keep up with and shopping close by. They had a few friends in the small town and that was enough for them. They could be happy here. Mary knew they would not be happy with her choices. She knew they wouldn't be happy about her getting married either so that was a good way to soften the blow of moving. Mary knew it was going to be difficult and she was not looking forward to it. She felt the longer she could put it off the less she would have to argue with anyone who found out that she was still dating Jack and that they had plans to marry. Mary was going to keep quiet for as long as possible.

Prom was coming up soon and Lisa was looking for a dress to wear. Mark promised to take Lisa even though he had already graduated and Lisa could not be happier. Lisa loved to get dressed up and go out. It was her way of showing Mark that she could dress up and knew how to act at parties despite her childhood of free choice and free spirited ways with her parents.

Lisa had always worked hard to know the proper etiquette required for each event. How to act, eat, dress and interact. Lisa was always looking for new information to keep up with whatever she needed to show she had class and poise. It didn't always work out but she never quite trying.

While out looking for her prom dress Lisa passed out on the floor. She was out with her friends, she had been feeling sick all day but she had never passed out before. Lisa was convinced it was due to not eating anything. She got something to eat and was still not feeling well. She thought maybe she was getting a cold but this feeling would not pass. Lisa's sister, Krystal suggested she take a pregnancy test. Lisa had not even considered being pregnant. That was a scary thought.

She knew she wanted Mark's babies but now his mother would know they had sex before they were married. Surely Mark's mother would not be happy if Lisa was pregnant. Neither would Mark. He always wanted everything in order. There was a time for everything and this was no time for a baby. Lisa took the test and found out she was pregnant. After talking with Mark they decided they would get married as soon as school was out. Lisa would most likely not be showing yet. She could finish school and they could move in together before she really started to show. It was not the path she thought she would take but she was happy they would be getting married, and getting married very soon.

Lisa was glad Mary would be around for her wedding but she knew she would miss Mary if she moved to the city. As happy as Lisa was to live in the small town with Mark and their babies. She could not help but wonder what life would be like in the city. She was happy Mary would get to go but a little disappointed she would be the one staying in the small town. She would miss Mary if she moved away. Jack and Mary would be there for Lisa and Mark's wedding and that would create the perfect place to announce their own plans to marry. They did not want kids until they moved and had jobs. They both knew if they had kids now it would be a lot harder to fit into life in the city. Life in the small town moved at a slower pace. There was more time to recover from setbacks if you had them. Also moving to the city they would have no family at all close by. Everyone they knew lived in the small town. They knew they had their work cut out for them but they were ready.   Mary just knew it would all work out.   She could just feel that it would be alright.

Now Lisa and Mary would be planning their weddings at the same time.   Both of them would be planning in a short amount of time while not spending a lot of money. If would be fun and they both knew they would not be around each other after Mary and Jack moved to the city.

Lisa and Mark's parents were not happy about the most recent news of Lisa's pregnancy.   That is the only thing they agreed on.   This was too much too soon for these two.   If they had only waited it could have been so much easier.   Now they would all have to make the best of the whole situation.   At least they both wanted to get married, move in together and start their family.   Lisa had managed to secure summer work at the county office and hopefully they would keep her on after summer. She would need to work while Mark worked seasonally to meet with the rules of becoming a full time firefighter.

Mark was not going to let anything get in the way of that reality. He had wanted it for so long and knew he would have to hang on to achieve his goal. He was not willing to accept anything less and Lisa knew that. She encouraged Mark's choices. They had already discussed the challenges they would face for at least the first few years.

Mary and Jack continued to save money. Jack was happy he found a partner that wanted to move to the city. He would have gone by himself but it would be a lot more fun and even easier together. They would get married before they moved. It would be something small.   Just a trip to the court house and a small reception afterwards. They were both okay with that so they would have more money for their move.

Housing would cost more than it did in the small town and they would need to get work as soon as possible. They both knew it would be a challenge but they were ready. They knew nothing would stop them, as long as they stayed focused on the long term goal of settling in the city.

Lisa and Mark had a quiet wedding ceremony with a small reception with friends and family afterwards. They rented the hall and after that party was over they would continue at their house with all their friends. They knew it would probably last all night. In the morning they would be off for three days in the mountains. It was not Lisa's first choice but she was happy they were at least getting away. Mark was convinced there was no reason to go anywhere. He thought it would be a waste of money. Lisa argued that soon it would be difficult for them to take any time

off after the baby was born and they should take it

while they could.

Three days was the absolute maximum amount of

days that would have even been an option.   It was fire

season and Mark would not miss even one day of

work.   He knew if he missed even one day he did not

want them to think he was not interested in working.

Every hour they made available to him he wanted to be

there to take.   Mark knew that was just one more way

to show his commitment.   He knew when they looked

at his history they would see his drive to be the best

and he would do nothing that would jeopardize that

record.

Lisa was only a few months pregnant so they would be

able to get married without having to tell everyone until

later that they were having a baby.   Their baby would

be born around Christmas.   Anyone doing the math would figure out she was pregnant when they got married but for now they could keep it quiet.   The fewer people who knew the better it would be for now.

Mary was happy for Lisa.   She knew she really wanted to get married and now she was.   Mary had finally told her grandparents she was going to marry Jack.   They were not happy but they knew once Mary turned eighteen there would be nothing they could do.   They told Mary's mom, Kathy.   As soon as she heard she made a trip to the small town to share with Mary her disappointment with her decision to marry Jack. Mary's mother knew she could be so much more in her life but Mary could never really take her mom seriously because she was always making such poor choices herself.   Mary had always hoped her mother would just decide one day that being her mom was important to her and she would stick around.

Most times she would talk to her one night and the next

morning she would be gone and it could be months

before they would hear from her again.   So

Mary never really worried too much about what her

mother thought.   She did want to make her mom

happy but knew that she would disappear and

reappear all the time and there was never any way to

tell how long it would be between times of being around

and gone. Mary knew they would all have to deal with

whatever she did because she was now eighteen and

able to make her own choices.   She knew she was

marrying Jack and moving to the city.   That was for

sure.

Chapter Five
Living Everyday

With things moving quickly Mary and Jack's wedding was a small but eventful celebration. They were married at the courthouse and had a reception afterwards. Jack was upset about guests that came to the reception. He accused Mary of being with one of her friend's boyfriends. Mary denied that anything had ever happened. They just happened to be the last two awake one weekend of partying and people like to make up stories. Especially when Jack was always so willing to believe anything negative or bad about anyone. Especially those close to him and especially Mary.

Mary had always been a target of Jack's rage. She spent a lot of time trying to smooth things out as they came up but Jack was just always looking for and making up trouble.   Although tempers flared and there

was shouting.   There was no physical fighting.   While

the party ended on a sour note the next morning

brought apologies and forgiveness for whatever

happened the night before.   There would be no

honeymoon for Mary and Jack.   They would be

leaving soon for the city and they were saving their

money.   They felt like they would be living a vacation

in the city and they wanted the best chance to make it

happen.   Even though everything was fine for Jack

and Mary, other people at the reception were worried

about the relationship and how it would progress.

Jack was aggressive and angry.   He would flip into

rages.   Yelling and striking out causing damage to

property and people.   Several of her friends and

family, especially her grandparents expressed concern

for her safety with Jack but Mary would assure them

she was fine and that she would be okay.   She wasn't

very convincing to others but Mary felt like she could fix

Jack.   That he would be nice if only she guided him.

She just felt that it would be okay.

Lisa and Mark were settling in after their trip.   It was

quiet and fun but now they were living together and

looking forward to having a baby.   Lisa graduated

from high school.   She was scheduled to work during

the summer and she was looking forward to it.   Lisa

loved to work a regular forty hour week job.   Not only

did it make her feel important.   She was earning

money.   That way she would have a little money

to spend on things for the house and the baby. They

would also be very busy as fire season for Mark was in

full swing and there was always a lot to do.   Mark was

working hard and looking good for future full time.

He was able to meet the requirements and

expectations of his supervisors.   Mark was committed

to be the best firefighter he could be and now he had a family to provide for.   He knew he was carrying a heavy load and he was not interested in failing.   That made Lisa happy too.

Mary and Jack were moving to the city.   They packed up the truck with everything they owned.   They would not be around for Lisa and Mark having their baby but Mary's grandparents would not let up about it being a mistake to move to the city.   They were convinced that Jack was not safe to live with.   That Mary should stay in the small town and go to just one year of college.   They honestly believed if Mary stayed in school she would see Jack for who he truly was and get as far away as she could before it was too late. This was all the more driving force for Mary to get out quickly and Jack only backed that up.   He knew the sooner they got to the city the better off they would be. Why should they hang around a place they never wanted to stay in.

Lisa would be able to work through the summer and Lisa and Mark would both be off for a couple months before the baby came.   That would make money tight when the baby came so they would need to work and save as much as they could while still paying all of their regular bills.   They can live simply for now but soon when Mark was hired on full time they would be able to do more.   Lisa looked forward to that time.

Chapter Six
Too Much...Anger Issues...

It was time for Jack and Mary to go. They would leave as soon as school started. That way there would be jobs open from students who went back to school. They packed up everything they needed and headed out. They were excited that the time was finally here.

Jack had been working for a local company who had family in the city. Jack had impressed his boss with his work ability and his boss had made calls to his family, living in the city, to let them know Jack would be moving to the city and that he was a good worker. This made it even better because now at least Jack already had a job lined up when they got there. That would give Mary a chance to find a place to live and set everything up before she looked for work.

Jack worked up until they were ready to leave and would start work the Monday following their arrival in the city. They had saved enough money to make rent for a few months. Now that Jack was working they would be able to rent a place and have money in savings just in case.

Lisa would be working until the baby was born. She could hardly wait. Her job had asked her to stay on after the summer. It was going to be so great. Lisa just knew once Mark's mom got to see what a great wife and now mother she would be, she would be happy that Mark chose Lisa. Lisa knew she could show Mark's mom that she would be the best at everything.

Jack and Mary found a place to rent within the first week. It was ready now so they could move in right away. They brought a few things with them but they would need to buy some things to fill their new place. Mary was excited but she had not been feeling well. She thought it might be the change in elevation or air quality. She was hoping it would pass but it hadn't yet. She went and got a home pregnancy test and found out she was pregnant.

This was not the time for a baby. Mary could just hear her grandparents now. "I knew this would happen and now you live so far away". When finding out the news Mary's grandparents made the decision to move closer to Mary. They were not happy about Mary being with Jack and now they had moved to the city and would be having a baby soon. Her grandparents wanted to be closer to Mary in case she needed them.

While Mary was not sure it would be a good idea for her grandparents to move close by. She was happy they would be close. As unhappy as they were with the choices Mary made they always tried to support her decisions and be close if she needed help.

Lisa was pregnant with a boy. While she wanted to name him Mark Junior. Mark would have no part of that. He wanted his son to have his own name and not have to grow up being a junior. They decided to name him Craig. They looked through all kinds of books and lists but both of them agreed on the baby's name. Lisa and Mark were both happy with their choice and looked forward to seeing their son for the first time.

They would be taking a child birth "what to expect" class. Mark's schedule would allow him to be at most of the classes, unless of course there was a call. He would have to be there to cover at a moment's notice. That was one thing that did not make Lisa happy. As much as she would try to plan around the times he would be available that could change at a moment's notice. He might have to leave and not be back for long periods of time. It was just the way it worked out. You would have to be available all the time, at a moment's notice, no matter what. Any of the times Mark could not go Lisa would go with her sister, Krystal. Lisa was hoping Mark would make it to all of the classes. She loved her sister Krystal but this was something she wanted to do with Mark. Mark really wanted to be there too, but Lisa knew work always came first. Lisa knew that was the best way to look at Mark's job and Mark knew it was the only way to look at his job.

Now that Mary knew she was pregnant she knew she needed to get a job quickly. She knew she wasn't too far along yet. The sooner she found work the better. Then she would be able to take maternity leave and go back to work.

She soon found a job at an office of a group of lawyers. Getting to know lawyers was something Mary learned about as a child going from lawyer to lawyer when her mother got too out of control and her grandparents felt they needed to protect her.

Her mother would go on crazy binges. Back and forth and sometimes that binge was to get Mary back from her parents. The problem was the binges never lasted very long and just as quickly she would be off on another binge, one that did not include Mary.

When Mary was really little her mother would take her to appointments to apply for charity programs. That way she looked more in need. After all she had a child. The problem was as soon as she received the benefit she would take Mary back to her grandparents and disappear again.

Mary's grandparents only wanted to keep Mary safe

and sometimes it would have to be done legally so Mary had found many friends with the office staff at law firms. It was now all working out to help her with her new job. This would be great.

Jack was not happy about, first of all, Mary being pregnant and now that she had a job. Jack did not want Mary to work at all but he thought for sure they would wait to have children. Jack was not even sure he wanted children. With Lisa getting pregnant a few months earlier they had talked about having babies and they had agreed they would wait. This was not in their plans and would now create a more difficult path to follow.

Mary was positive she would keep any baby they created. She loved Jack too much to let go of their own flesh and blood. Although not planned they would be having a baby and they would need all the money they could to make ends meet and live like they wanted.   Both Jack and Mary did agree on that.

Lisa and Mark were getting things ready for the new baby's arrival.   They had agreed they would name their son Craig.   They both really liked the name. While Lisa would prefer Mark Craig she knew it was as close as she was going to get to a junior.   As much as Mark was clear in his career path he did not want to push his life choices on his son.   He felt his parents had already planned his life and he had no say in the matter.   He wanted his own son to choose his own path and decide for himself what career he wanted to choose.   He was always grateful for his opportunity to have this path laid out before him.   He did not want that for his son and he was making that clear.

It was not long now and they would have their new baby.   Even though they were worried about having a baby at such a young age.   They were both extremely

excited.   They were looking forward to seeing their

own baby and watching him grow.   Lisa knew it was

going to be hard to leave him at a babysitter while she

worked.   She enjoyed working and knew that it would

be better in the long run for all of them.   When Mark

was off season he would be home to take care of

Craig.   That was all the more reason for Lisa to go

back to work right away.

Mary was getting their house ready for a new baby too.

She and Lisa talked on a regular basis and shared

doctor visit stories.   Mary was having a few difficulties

through her pregnancy but the office she worked at

was willing to work with her.   It was a big office and

they told her they would do whatever they needed to

cover for her while she was pregnant.   Her co-workers

really enjoyed being around Mary but as always people

were afraid of the power Jack seemed to have over

Mary.

A few times Jack had made clear that Mary will do what he wants regardless of what other people think or do. Mary loved Jack a lot and she truly believed that Jack would be a great husband and father.   The problem was no one else did, not even Jack.   He knew that Mary would do all that would be necessary for their kids and she would work full time as well.   He was not willing to work through any of the details, he made that clear from the start.   Mary knew that was what he said but she believed when they had kids he would want to be involved.   It was time for Lisa to have the baby. She would deliver at the hospital and stay just a couple of days if everything went okay.   Lisa was scared but excited.   She knew as soon as she had this baby her life would change forever.

She knew she would be forever linked to Mark.   His

mother would have to accept her now. Lisa was sure she would be a part of the family once Craig was born. As unhappy as Mark's mother was about a grandchild now, she was excited to see the new baby and the fact that it was a boy made it all the better. Mark would carry on the family name with this baby.

Mary would not be able to come to the small town to see their new baby. They were planning a trip to the small town but it would have to be after Mary had her baby and that was if everything went well. Mary had to stay off her feet often when she was pregnant.

While Mary was sure Jack wanted to be a good father and husband the fact that he wasn't even trying was taking a toll on Mary. Even if she did not want to admit it. There did seem to be a link between Jack's outbursts and calls for bed rest. Mary refused to budge. She just knew any day Jack would turn the corner and be the best dad and husband ever to walk the face of the earth and no one could make her believe anything different.

During this time people close to Mary were becoming more and more concerned for her safety. Jack could become very scary in a short amount of time. He seemed to get upset about everything. It did not matter who was around or what Mary was doing.

While Jack would blow up quickly, he would always apologize later and promise never to get that angry again. Then he would buy some kind of gift to apologize with. It was always something Mary wanted but knew they could not afford. Jack would always find a way to get what he needed to get. Even if he had to work seven days a week. Mary would always have to keep the house running smoothly and she continued to work so if something did happen she would be able to keep up with the bills.

Lisa and Mark welcomed Craig home and worked at creating their new family routine. Craig was a good baby. He only cried when he needed something. Like when he was hungry or wet. He slept through the night and Lisa and Mark were so happy with him. He was a lot of work but he was a fun baby. Lisa and Mark were so proud of him. Even though Mark's mother did not like to admit it out loud, she was impressed with the commitment and energy both Mark and Lisa put towards doing everything they needed to do for their new family. They both wanted to make this work and it showed.

Even with all the bed rest Mary was required to get everything was looking good for Mary and Jack's baby. They found out they were having a boy and they would name him Chris. Mary chose the name and Jack agreed.

Jack had no interest in any part of this child or any other kids they would have.   He felt like that was something Mary wanted and she would need to do whatever was involved with taking care of them.   Mary knew she was on her own for now but honestly believed as soon as Jack saw their son he would want to be involved.   At least a little bit, she hoped.

Mary was getting closer to having Chris and she was afraid that maybe Jack would not even show up when she was in labor.   Let alone participate.   Mary could always invite someone from work, just in case Jack could not make it.   She just knew if she did it would end up badly.   It was never good to have Jack around anyone from her work anymore.   They all believed Jack was abusive and Mary would be better off without him. Mary always told them they were wrong about Jack.   He just had a lot on his mind, or he

was just looking out for her.   Just keeping her safe

from getting hurt.   The more and more it happened the

less believable it was to listen to Mary's excuses.

Mary always felt that everything would be fine and Jack

would never actually really hurt her.   She had been

lucky, for now,   that she was quick on her feet and

knew when she should disappear and stay away for

awhile.   That was, of course, if she could get away.

Lisa would talk to Mary regularly and she too was

worried.   Lisa knew after Mary had her baby she

would have to look out for herself and a baby and she

knew how much Mark helped her out.   She could not

imagine doing it by herself and with no family around.

Mary wasn't worried.   She knew she could do it by

herself and her grandparents were still fairly close.

She just knew Jack would pitch in, at least one day.

As time grew closer for Mary to have Chris, Jack

seemed more and more distant.   Jack always thought Mary secretly wanted to get pregnant and maybe it wasn't even his baby.   Jack would think "who knows what Mary does when she was not around him." There was very little time Mary was not with Jack and certainly not long enough to have any kind of relationship with anyone besides Jack.   What little time was not spent with Jack,   Mary was busy doing things Jack expected to be done.

Whatever the case, Mary knew Jack was the father she would not be with anyone else and she was trying hard to prove that to Jack.   He just never acted like he believed it.   No matter how hard Mary tried. She was fighting a losing battle.   Jack did seem to enjoy making Mary feel uncomfortable or overloaded. He seemed to do it on purpose.   He was constantly trying to keep her always worried something was just not right.   Always trying to create work and chaos.

When Chris was born Jack was nowhere to be found. He took off when Mary started to feel contractions and did not come back for three days. Mary had no idea where he went and why he left but that left her alone to have the baby and Jack made no excuses for it. He did what he wanted, when he wanted and that was that. Mary had a friend from work with her and her grandparents came as soon as she called. They had taken classes together but Jack said he freaked out when she started having contractions and he just couldn't do it. Mary was unhappy that Jack was not there but was glad when he did come home. She did not want to raise this baby by herself. Even if she had to do everything she just wanted Jack to be around. The only reason he went to the classes was to make sure Mary was not going to hook up with any of the other fathers. Mary still believed if only she could show him how good it would be if they were a happy family working together.   Even when Jack did come back he was really not interested in Chris at all.   He had no patience for anything that had to do with Chris. Even though Chris was a good baby, Jack would get angry when Mary would have to do anything to take care of him.   He would go crazy when Chris would cry. Even if it was just for a minute.   Mary would have to take Chris for a ride in the car to avoid Jack's ranting about the baby crying.   Even though Mary spent a lot of time trying to keep Jack happy she knew Jack would come around soon.   He just needed time.   Time to adjust to having a baby around.   Mary was willing to do everything so she could make that happen.

Lisa and Mark were enjoying their new baby.   Lisa would be going back to work and Mark was off season. He would stay home with Craig.   Lisa was struggling with leaving Craig but she knew at least he would be home with Mark.   She didn't know what she would do if she had to put Craig in daycare.   She knew that day would come but at least for now while he was little he would be home with Mark.   Lisa worked close by and could come home for lunch which made it nice.

Mark was good with Craig.   He was working hard to be a good dad.   He talked a lot about how good Craig would be at sports and how many games they would win.   Baseball, football, any sport would make Mark happy.   Lisa did have concerns for her son.   What if he didn't want to play sports?   But he was young now and Lisa was happy that Mark was willing to stay home with Craig.   She was happy they could work together and one day Mark would be hired on full time and they would be able to do more things.   Then Lisa might be able to spend more time with her son.

Just when Mary was settling in with their new baby she found out she was pregnant again.   No one was thrilled. People were actually upset. How could she think of bringing another child in when the one they had was just starting to settle in and become a part of their every day. Mary was surprised it had happened so fast but she was always strong in her belief that we all pay to play and any type of sex had the possibility of pregnancy. When that happened, as far as Mary was concerned, there would be a baby. Jack saw it as a way to control Mary's time and possibly get her away from working all together. The best part of Jack spending most of his time away from home was he did spend a lot of time at work. He was doing well. He was making good money and moving up quickly. Mary could easily stop working and they would be fine.

Mary did want to be home with the kids but she did enjoy working and sometimes when Jack would get angry the only thing that helped her was being expected to be at work or having people she worked with around her. Mary had a comfort that she did not want to let go of because she worked. As much as Jack pressured her, that was one thing she was not willing to give up. Even with a second pregnancy and baby.

Lisa was happy with the way things were going for her, Mark and baby Craig. She could not imagine expanding her family yet. With news of Mary being pregnant with her second baby. Lisa was happy with the one they had. She did think about one day down the road having a girl but for now it was working out for them growing into their everyday life. Lisa knew they would have plenty of time for more kids later.

Chapter Seven
Moving Back

Mary knew having two kids was going to be a lot of work and more money with added expenses.   She was working hard to show Jack that they could do this, as much as Jack wanted to keep Mary at home.   He was not really sure that Mary was pregnant with his child.   Jack somehow felt it happened too fast.   Therefore it must not be his baby.   It depended on the day you were talking to Jack whether Chris was his or not.   Sometimes he would say, Chris was his and other days he would act as if he knew Chris was not his.

This new baby was different.   Jack was constantly badgering Mary about her whereabouts when she got pregnant with this second baby.   Mary just felt like it was more of the same but it did feel like Jack did not believe that this was his baby.   It seemed to be more up in her face about this baby.

Jack would say horrible things about what he would do if he found out this baby was not his.   Mary knew these babies both belonged to Jack but sometimes the things Jack would say would make her wonder if that was how he truly felt.   Mary knew she would have to be careful.   That was all, she knew Jack would come around.   In the meantime she was doing pretty good keeping up with everything.

While this pregnancy was easier than the first one Mary still had her bed rest time.   She would have to stay in bed for a few days but they did not last as long as the times during her first pregnancy.   Mary found out they were having another boy.   They would name him Brock.   Mary was busy getting stuff ready for Brock.   They did have stuff from Chris but he was, for the most part, still using his crib and other stuff. Mary and Jack would buy all new stuff for Brock. Jack was okay with that as long as she left him alone.

Lisa was worried about Mary but she was busy working and enjoying their new baby and way of life. Now that they were married and parents. Mark was adjusting well to his new role as a daddy. They both seemed to fit together in their role as parents. They were young and did still enjoy getting together with friends and partying together.

Most of their friends were not old enough but it did not matter. They would get together at each other's houses just like they had in high school only now many of their friends had places of their own or more time available in their parent's houses. As their parents would leave them to care for the house while they were away. They had been doing that for a while. As they got older they realized that it was much easier to

keep damages to a minimum at their parties and to

know when the owners of the house would be returning

so they could continue this practice.   The less

damage, the less trouble.   If all they needed to do was

clean up they were willing to do that.

So with all those times of partying there were many

stories about things that happened while they were

intoxicated.   Some true, some not true and surely

some that had been seriously exaggerated to create a

better story.   Lisa enjoyed partying just like Mark did

but Lisa continued to party in excess and leave herself

open to being included in many crazy situations which

Mark did not care for.   Mark did not want people

talking about him or talking about his wife.   For Lisa,

as much as she wanted to set a great example she had

very low tolerance for handling her partying.   Lisa just

did not know when to quit and Mark always wanted to

throw these stories in Lisa's face, all the time.

Mark just felt that Lisa would always do more if he was not around and many times he would leave early or take care of Craig if he woke up. Most times Lisa was not capable of taking care of herself after partying, let alone Craig.

When they were partying, most times she would not even hear him or pay attention to him if he needed something. So Mark would end up caring for him or leaving to pick him up if he was sick or needed something.

Mark couldn't help but listen to the stories people had about Lisa. When he would talk to Lisa she would apologize and tell Mark she would not party as much. As hard as Lisa tried and wanted to she did not always leave when she should and things would happen or people would talk and Lisa often times was somehow involved.   Even if sometimes it was just that she happened to be there.   She would party as often as she could and because they had always partied together it had never been a big deal before.   Mark knew they were both young but Lisa needed to figure it out because Mark was already getting tired of it.   Lisa would talk to Mary about Mark but never really said it was any big deal.   While Mary would always tell Lisa everything was great and that Jack helped out all the time.

While Lisa listened to what Mary would say she did not feel that Jack would change overnight and Lisa knew the restrictions their own one child put on their own life. She knew it had to be much more with two kids.   Yet Mary always acted like it was no big deal and things were great with her and Jack.

Mary was scared to tell people how Jack acted to her

and Chris.   Now with the new baby coming she knew it would most likely be more of the same.   Mary still felt like at any moment he would change his ways and be happy to be married and proud to be a father of two beautiful boys.

Mary felt that once Brock was born Jack would turn around and be the best husband and father he could be.   No matter how much she hoped it would happen, it had not happened yet.   Mary knew she would need to keep up the stories of how great it was.   It was just easier than admitting it was not good and Mary was getting to be more and more afraid of Jack.

She never thought he would be aggressive to a baby but he was aggressive sometimes and she could not always see it coming or avoid it.   If Jack was angry you would know, it did not matter who you are.   Mary just hoped with two boys he would be able to see what a good wife and mother she was.

It wasn't always the way Jack saw it. While he wasn't willing to help at all he was certainly willing to share his opinions or choices for Mary to follow.   Mary was always trying.   It was just really difficult to keep up with all his suggestions while he just watched her care for Chris.

Jack had no interest in feeding, changing or caring for kids and made it clear that it would not be something he would do.   Mary knew that is what he said.   She just did not believe that he would not take care of him if he needed something.   At the same time, she wasn't interested in leaving Jack alone with Chris to find out.   Jack would not even attempt to keep Chris by himself for any amount of time anyway.   So there didn't seem to be much of a chance he would even be given the opportunity to find out.

Mary and Jack welcomed their second son Brock a little bit different than Chris.   Even though Jack wanted nothing to do with the coaching or helping of the baby's birth.   He wanted only to see that the baby that was born looked like him and know that there was no mix up or switching out of babies.   Besides, he would know by looking at this baby whether it was his or not.   Jack wanted to be sure from the beginning. Mary did not care why, she was just happy that Jack would be there.

Even after Jack witnessed Brock being born it was worse with two now than it had ever been with one. Jack had no tolerance for Mary, let alone two babies.   Brock had a hard time keeping formula down. He would throw up a lot and cry a lot.   Doctors told Mary it sometimes took a while for some babies to find out which formula was best for them and the process was completely within normal limits for a new baby.

Jack did tend to favor Chris if pushed to choose between the two but really had very little interest in either one of them.   He just wanted Mary to keep them quiet.   Nothing would get him as fired up as crying babies.   Mary tried her best but there were times she just couldn't make it stop.   Mary just hoped it would all work itself out and Jack would step up.   She was tired and still trying to work and take care of her growing family.   Mary knew if things didn't change she was not sure how long she would be able to hang on.

Lisa and Mark decided to take a trip to see Mary and Jack.   It would have to be a short trip.   They would go for a long weekend.   It was the end of season and Mark would be off work soon so that would be the time to go.   That would give Lisa time to request the time off.   Even if it was going to be just a few days.   They would leave early Thursday morning and drive back on Tuesday night.   That way they could stay for six days and only miss two days of work.

Lisa and Mary were excited to see each other. Mary and Jack had just moved to a three bedroom house so there would be plenty of room for Lisa, Mark and Craig to stay at their house. They would be able to check out the city while seeing old friends.

While Lisa knew Mark would never move. She was always trying to push Mark out of his comfort zone. She was always asking him "what if we just did this…" or "what is we went there…". Mark was rigid in his goals and thinking. He had to have it all spelled out long before he would actually attempt it. While Lisa would just jump into the middle of it and make it work. Even though Lisa knew that way could get you in trouble, it was fun sometimes. Even if she did love the security of a job well planned. Mark would occasionally step out but not for long.

118

Lisa and Mark went to visit Mary and Jack for the holidays. They were able to show off Craig and meet Chris and Brock. It was fun seeing each other again. So many things had changed in the last couple of years. While Lisa knew they would have more children she was willing to wait. She always felt there was just never enough money. With Mark having on and off seasons, when he was working they would be able to start buying things they wanted. Then the season would end and it would be time to cut back and make the best of what they already had.

Lisa wanted Craig to have everything he would or could want. Lisa always wanted her kids to have whatever they wanted and that all they had was new and not someone else's old hand me downs. She knew Mark would make that happen. She just liked to nudge him occasionally.

The visit went well.   It was good to see Mary and Jack. The boys were adorable and it was nice to see how they had all changed.   Mary and Jack wanted to show Lisa and Mark the city and how much there was to do. They showed Lisa and Mark all kinds of places that they had in the city.   It was like they were kids again but there was so many more places to go.

Mary's grandparents, Joe and Dottie kept the kids for the times they wanted to go out without kids.   They were all little but Craig and Chris played well together and Brock was doing better with formula as he was getting older.   This was only after they went through several different formulas to find one that worked the best.   Mary was nervous but the doctor did say it would work itself out and Mary knew it would just take time.

Lisa was so glad they did not have any problems with

Craig.   He ate well and was growing as he should.

Lisa and Mark were both very grateful Craig was

healthy and growing on target.

Mary was so busy keeping up with everything.   She

had gone back to work as soon as her doctor would

release her.   Mary did love her kids but she really

enjoyed working and would spend as much time at

work as she could.   She loved her kids but Jack was

so mean.   It was hard to feel good about anything she

did while Jack was always there to remind her of how

much time she wasted or that she was doing

everything wrong.   Jack did make sure to remind her

again and again as often as he could.

As much as Mary loved Jack this attitude would wear

her down and she would start to believe all the awful

things Jack would say.   He could be so mean and

he did not care who saw him or heard him.   Mary

would try not to be out in public or with work friends around Jack.   Jack had made so many scenes about such small incidences.   More than one person had talked to Mary about his behavior or tone of voice, with concerns for her safety.   Mary would just dismiss these concerns and tell them not to worry.   It was not like that and Jack just had difficulty communicating with others.   Still many friends and family would worry about Mary's safety and even more now with two babies.   Surely that would just add fuel to the fire.

Even though Jack was usually making Mary's days unbearable they had a good visit while Lisa, Mark and Craig were staying with them.   They were able to spend time together and just talk about how things used to be and how much had changed for all of them. It was a lot of fun but the end of the visit came quickly and Lisa, Mark and Craig headed back home to the small town.

Lisa would be back to work and Mark would be helping

out his parents. It seemed they would always have a

list of chores for Mark. Either that or it would be the

way to get him over to their house and once he was

there it was easy to convince him to stay. Mark would

always do as his mother asked, and his mother did ask

a lot.

Most times Lisa didn't really care too much but she had

not been feeling well and it did seem like he was

spending a lot of time away from home. Lisa was

feeling tired and she was working while Mark was off

season. After not feeling well for awhile Lisa decided

she should take a pregnancy test. She found out she

was pregnant but she was afraid to tell Mark.

She knew how much Mark did not want another child

right now. While Mark was happy they had Craig.

Mark knew two kids would be twice as difficult as things

were now.   The only thing that would make him happy is that Lisa would not be drinking while she was pregnant.

Mark did not like that Lisa enjoyed drinking so much. He wanted her to always leave when he left, no matter how long he stayed.   Lisa, however, would leave when she was ready.   Not when Mark was ready. After all they always partied with all their friends from high school.   This is exactly what Mark did not like.

According to Mark, Lisa needed to show all their friends she was with him now and that they would always do things together.   Lisa liked to be last to leave the party and Mark was more likely to leave early.   Mark would always leave before everything got out of control.   Lisa did know she did not party while she was pregnant.   She always wanted to give her baby the best chance.

Mark had been so matter of fact about having one child. Lisa was not sure she wanted to see how he was going to react. She did know she would have to tell him so she decided to plan a night out and she would tell him then, what could he say. They were married and they did talk about having more kids. This second baby was just sooner than expected. She knew Mark would be alright in the long run but it was telling him that it was happening. Now, that was the scary part.

Lisa set up a night out and told Mark. While he was not extremely happy he knew that they did run a risk of getting pregnant and Mark believed Lisa would not get pregnant on purpose. They found out she was having a girl. Lisa was so happy she was having a girl. Mark was happy too. They had a boy and now they would have a girl. They could be done. That way they could agree to take steps to end the possibility of another pregnancy. Either Lisa would have her tubes tied or Mark would have a vasectomy. That way there would be no question about future babies.

While Lisa was happy she was having a girl, she was not so sure she wanted this to be her last baby. She did not know why but Mark had made it clear that this would be his last child. Even if he was the one to have a vasectomy. He made that perfectly clear. While Lisa knew he meant what he said she felt like he would change his mind later and they would have more kids. She knew they would have more kids later but for now they were having a little girl. They would call her Connie.

Mark was working out well at the fire house and Lisa knew it would not be long before he would be hired on full time. As much as Lisa liked to work she did look forward to the day she would be able to stay home with the kids.   She liked doing stuff with Craig and was a little jealous of the time Mark was allowed to have with Craig.   Lisa tried to spend as much time as she could with Craig but Craig said his first words with Mark, sat up by himself for the first time with Mark.   Lisa always seemed to be working when Craig would reach his many milestones.

Lisa was trying really hard not to miss the "firsts".   She worked close to home so she could come home on her lunch hour and was only a few minutes away if she needed to get home quick.   Mark could and did get called out to work at any time while he was off season. It didn't happen a lot but it did happen.

While Mark was accepting the fact they would soon have two children, he was not ready for his mother to know just yet.   He knew he would have to tell her and it would have to be soon but he wanted to wait as long as he possibly could before telling her.

While Mark's mother was concerned when she did find out, she was very happy with the progress Mark had been able to make up to this point towards his future. She wanted to continue to encourage Mark to meet his goals. No matter what, Mark knew he would and he just wanted to make his mother believe it would be with Lisa. Mark was sure he did not want to start over with someone new. He wanted his family to work out the first time.

While Mark's mom had not always been a fan of Lisa's. She had stopped being so mean to her. As soon as Craig was born she knew they were linked by blood for life. She knew she would have to be friends with Lisa to see the grandkids. So she was willing to keep the peace to see her grandchildren. While Lisa knew they had a rocky past she was sure she accepted her now.   After all Lisa gave Mark a son and soon

enough a daughter.   The perfect family they would be

now.

Lisa had little to no trouble carrying her babies.   She

was a little more tired with this pregnancy simply

because she was trying to spend as much time with

Craig as she could, while still working full time and of

course keeping up with her friends.   Even if she wasn't

drinking while she was pregnant she would still

hang out with her friends every weekend.   She did

leave sometimes with Mark but a lot of times she would

stay because Mark was often ready to leave long

before Lisa was ready.

Mary was missing her life in the small town.   Living

with Jack was taking a toll on her and she knew if

things were to go bad with Jack she would not be able

to make enough money to cover their expenses.   She

would have to move back to the small town.

Things were close and easier to get to there. She also had more family and friends in the small town. They had gotten to know a lot of people while living in the city but most would come and go. They would either move on or move back to their small towns. A lot of the friends they did have were Jack's friends and their wives from work.

Mary was hesitant to bring her friends from work around. Jack would always try to make trouble and sometimes it was difficult for Mary to explain. While she still loved Jack a lot she was tired and she was tired of waiting for Jack to step up and help out. Sometimes when she would look at Jack she did not even recognize him. He had such a cold stare. Sometimes it seemed he just had no compassion for anyone. Most of the time his aggression was directed at Brock. Jack always tried to make Brock feel like he ruined everything when he was born.

Jack was not very good with one child but now with two children he was not willing to add to his responsibilities. He always felt like Mary got pregnant too fast for it to be his. Chris and Brock did look alike but Mary was blond and so was Chris while Brock had dark hair just like Jack, which made it even more difficult to understand why he would not accept Brock as his own. Sometimes it seemed that Jack was so cold-blooded. It seemed he would think nothing of chopping them all up into little pieces. As the boys got older it became increasingly obvious that Jack was capable of just about anything when he was mad. Mary was not sure how much longer they would all be safe. She just tried not to think about it and tried to keep Jack happy. Mary had talked to Lisa and found out she was pregnant with a girl. She was happy for Lisa and knew now they would have a boy and a girl. That is

what Lisa always wanted.   She also knew that

Mark was okay with that being the end of the babies for

them.   But Lisa was not so sure she was done.   She

always wanted a lot of kids.   Just because she got her

boy and then a girl did not mean it was over for them.

While Mark was done, he was ready to put an end

to having kids, and for Mark, that was that.   Lisa had

Connie just like she had Craig with little complication

and Connie was a beautiful healthy baby girl.   Lisa

and Mark were so happy everything went well and that

Connie was finally here.   Just a short stay in the

hospital and Lisa and Connie were home.   Lisa took

off work for the first eight weeks of Connie's life.

While she was off work she talked to Mary a lot.   Mary

was having a difficult time keeping up.   Jack was so

mean and she spent so much time trying to keep him

happy while also taking care of the boys.

Chapter Eight
What Is Really Going On?

Mary called Lisa to tell her that she had just found out she was pregnant again and Jack was not interested in any part of her or the kids anymore. While Jack claimed "all Mary did was drink" Mary would drink more to forget about how angry Jack got about everything.

She knew with another baby it would be even more difficult to manage things at home. While Jack was doing well at work, Mary continued to work for the lawyers and made good money herself. Mary was tired and afraid. She just could not predict what would set Jack off. It could even be nothing. If Mary did not pay enough attention to Jack or paid too much attention to him.

Mary just never knew and Jack seemed to enjoy

making her uncomfortable. Which freaked Mary out even more.

How could someone who said they loved you so much be so mean? You could see his face light up when he saw something getting to someone. He tried a lot to make that happen. He seemed to have no mercy and he would target his favorites but was generally mean and rude to everyone. It was finally just getting to the point Mary could no longer take it. She knew it would be hard with three kids all by herself but she knew it was too difficult to continue on the way things were going now.

Even though this third baby was going to be difficult, Mary found out she was having a girl. After talking with Jack Mary found out he was not interested in being with Mary anymore either. He told Mary he was not interested in being any part of the family unless he was left alone and allowed to do what he wanted.

While Mary was glad Jack was being up front about

what he was willing to do and not do.   She knew

she was looking for a partner and family.   She was not

looking to be a single parent who was controlled by a

partner who would have no interest in being involved

with the family.   Jack was looking to be left alone,

being allowed to do what he wanted, when he wanted,

while still controlling everyone else in the house.

Mary and Jack agreed they would move back to the

small town as soon as the new baby was born.   Jack

wanted out and Mary knew if she was going to raise

these kids by herself it would be easier to do it in the

small town where family and friends were closer.   At

least Jack was willing to do that for Mary.   That did

give her a little hope.   Jack did make it perfectly clear it

was only for him to get away not for Mary or the

kids.

While Jack did have somewhat of a relationship with Chris, he felt no obligation to have a relationship with Brock or with the new baby girl. With this pregnancy Mary had gone in to it knowing she would be on her own. Jack was not interested and Mary knew if she was going to do it alone she would make all the decisions. She would decide where she would go to have the baby and she would decide the baby's name and what furniture they would have for the baby's room. After all, this baby was a girl and she would need pretty and precious furniture. While the boys furniture was definitely for boys.

Mary and Jack named this baby Angel. She was a beautiful little girl. She was always so quiet. Never crying for longer than just a second. Just enough to let you know she needed something. This made it so much easier for Mary. She was so busy with her growing family and now they were moving. A lot of work to be done.   A lot of plans to be made.   Jack

was just working a lot and doing as little as possible to

help with the move.

Lisa was excited Mary and Jack were moving back.

While Jack and Mary had decided to move back so

Jack could be on his own.   Mary did not share that

with anyone.   She just told them with three kids it was

hard to live and work in the city, daycare was

expensive and it was hard to find one that was good

and would last.

Lisa was happy because she really missed hanging

out with Mary.   Now their kids would be growing up

together.   Mark was not as excited.   There was really

no connection between Mark and Jack.   Mark did not

like the way Jack was always so confrontational.   It

seemed like he was always looking for a fight.   This

was just not Mark's style.   He was really not an

aggressive person.   Mark may have a specific way he wanted things to be but he was never physically aggressive.   He might yell a lot and express his dislike of a situation but never physically violent.   While it seemed Jack would flip into a violent rage at the drop of a hat.   Mark also knew that Mary liked to drink a lot. Mark was not a fan of Mary or Jack and was not as excited for them to return to the small town.

Regardless of who was happy about it and who wasn't Mary and Jack were moving back with their three kids. Only Mary and Jack knew they would separate as soon as they got settled back in the small town.

Mary was fed up and tired of trying to please Jack. Mary knew while Jack was making good money in the city he would not make as much in the small town. Besides being a smaller market,   Jack had treated people badly in the small town.   Mary knew she would need to get back and distance herself from Jack as quickly as she could. She knew for the safety of the kids and herself that would be the best for all of them. Now that Jack and Mary had decided they no longer wanted to be together what little sympathy Jack had given them before was quickly disappearing.

Jack could be so mean when he called himself her husband. Now that they decided to separate he was ruthless to her and the kids. Mary was scared and just kept trying to get things done so she could get out with the kids and be safer. She knew Jack would hold a grudge about whatever he made up in his head and there was not a lot she could do about that. All she could do now was focus on getting herself situated back in the small town.

Lisa and Mark, while their relationship was less violent they were struggling themselves. The responsibility of two children while they were so young was taking its toll on them as well.   Mark was angry with Lisa about how social she was and Lisa struggled with Mark's rigid demeanor. For Mark it was one way, one plan and to stick to it no matter what.   Lisa was more free-spirited and spontaneous.   While Mark would go into things with a plan Mary would not always stick to the plan and was easily distracted.   This infuriated Mark and they had many heated arguments about Lisa's flippant attitude.   Lisa would argue that Mark was too rigid and there was no wiggle room for her. She did try to follow Mark's plan but would be having fun and not want it to stop.   Everyday life had so many demands on her time Lisa would just like to let go sometimes and forget about the plan.   This is one thing Mark could just not understand.   Overall Lisa and Mark were both good parents.   Mark was just very strict in his ideas and parenting style.

While Lisa was more easy going and open to different ideas. Lisa's sister, Krystal was getting divorced. She had her son, David before Craig was born and she had been married to Mike for three years. Mike decided Krystal was not the wife for him. He wanted full custody of David. While Krystal was okay with joint custody, she was not interested in giving up custody of David.

She told Mike they would need to reach an agreement regarding David. Clearly neither one of them would be walking away. So now Lisa was spending more time with her sister Krystal. Mark seemed to be angry with Krystal. Lisa tried to explain to Mark that Krystal was just going through a difficult time right now. With her divorce and custody issues she was working through a lot and it would just be for a little while. Mark did want to understand but he was not happy about it.

Mary and Jack moved back to the small town. They found a nice house just outside of town and started looking for jobs. Mary got a job with the county rather quickly. She had worked there during summers while she was in high school. Jack was picking up jobs here and there but nothing full time just yet. They were settling in and making the best of their situation.

Mary and Jack decided to move into the same place for now until Mary was set up with the kids, then Jack would move out. The kids were young enough to go with the changes without much problem. They were back in the small town and fell right back into the crowd they went to high school with. While things had definitely changed. Some had kids, some went on to college and others had moved away. Those that could were still around and Mary and Jack were settling in. Mary was drinking a lot more than usual and neither Mary or Jack were interested in hanging

out with each other.

Chapter Nine
New Families Defined

Lisa just wanted everyone to get along. This did seem unlikely, but that is what Lisa wanted. Mary would usually start drinking early so she would pass out early. Mark would leave early most times too.

This left Lisa and Jack up late together partying a lot. They spent many nights just talking and reconnecting with each other. They would share marriage and kid stories. Lisa and Mary had talked about Jack's violent outbursts. While Lisa had seen a small amount of these outbursts years ago in high school, she had no idea about how often and how violent he had been.

Of course Jack minimized his aggressive behavior. He claimed it was only due to Mary's excessive drinking and his belief of multiple affairs. Mary had grown tired of trying to defend herself from the accusations and had simply left him to believe what he wanted. Which left Jack open to create multiple scenarios in his head.

While Lisa and Mary were friends, good friends, Lisa could not help but believe the horrible stories Jack was telling her about their time in the city. With Jack's version, he was always the one who was left with the kids, left to pay the bills or left with all the responsibility. Which could not have been farther from the truth but it is what he filled Lisa's head with.

Lisa and Mary were working together and as time went by Lisa was getting angrier and angrier with Mary. Lisa believed the stories Jack was telling her and she believed everything Jack said. Lisa was not interested in what Mary had to say. On several nights Lisa and Jack would talk all night. They would not go home and Mary and Mark were asking questions.

While Mary knew it was only a matter of time before her and Jack split up.   She did not want to be the wife people were whispering about.   Mary confronted Jack and accused him of cheating.   Jack assured her he had not cheated and he had just gotten too drunk to drive and had passed out and when he woke up he drove home.   While Mary did not believe him there was really nothing she could do.   She was too busy with the kids and working full time to spend that much time on what Jack was doing.

Lisa was struggling with the information Jack was sharing with her.   It pushed Lisa to think about her own life and marriage.   Lisa was not sure Mark was the one for her.   She knew that looking in to someone's life revealed the truth about who they really are and that when you first meet someone things may seem different and only after spending everyday with them do you realize the truth.

Lisa knew Mark was seriously controlled by his mother. While things were better since Lisa had the kids. Lisa felt she always had to walk on egg shells with Mark's mother. She would constantly compare Lisa to past girlfriends or even other women that she believed were such a better match for Mark. Lisa did not like to admit it but it was clearly taking a toll on her and their marriage.

According to Jack, he was working so hard to be a good dad and not being allowed to. Lisa started to believe the stories Jack told and felt like she could raise her kids and Jack's kids and everything would be great. Lisa made the decision to move out with the kids into her own apartment. She did not want to spend any more time with Mark.   She told Mark she

needed space and that she was just trying to sort

things out in her head.

While Mark was surprised at Lisa's request he agreed.

He was starting to believe things had moved way to

fast and maybe Lisa was not the one for him

either.   They just seemed to have different priorities

and Mark was not sure they would ever be on the same

page.   He was not happy about it but he knows there

is problems and cannot disagree with this plan.   The

kids would go back and forth as Mark is off work.   With

Lisa in her own place Jack was spending more and

more time there.

Mary was fed up with Jack not coming home and told

him to move out.   Jack packed his things and went to

Lisa's house.   Lisa was telling both Mark and Jack that

they were the only one she wanted.   Lisa was not sure

which one she wanted to be with. Mark had not been hired on full time yet but he would be soon. Jack was not working right now but her feelings for him were growing every day. With it being a small town everyone knows everyone's business. It did not take long for it to come out that Jack was living with Lisa. Mark was furious and immediately filed for divorce. Lisa is not willing to give up custody and they worked out an agreeable visitation schedule for the kids.

While Lisa is sad her marriage is over she is excited at the thought of a new life with Jack. If there had been any aggressive situations between Lisa and Jack she was not talking about them. She was in love with Jack even though she did still have love for Mark and the simpler times when they were a family.

Mary filed for divorce from Jack and they struggled more with the separation and visitation schedule.

Mary feared for her children when they were with Jack. Even though Jack was with Lisa, Mary knew Jack was capable of serious violence. She had seen it and been the target of it for many years.

While Mary was hurt by her friend being with Jack she was worried for Lisa too. She had told Lisa on several occasions, "You can have him. I don't want him". Everyone believed Mary was just bitter and angry that Jack had moved on and with one of her good friends. To say they were best friends would probably be more than the truth but they had been good friends for a long time.

While Mary and Jack's divorce was taking longer than Lisa and Mark's had there were many weekends that Jack did not see the kids. The oldest boys, Chris and Craig were five this year and starting kindergarten. While Mark was actively participating in Craig and

Connie's lives as often as he could. Chris had to listen to Craig talk about what fun they had playing sports and games in the front yard with Chris's dad. This was hard for Chris to listen to. He was not seeing his dad as much and now had to hear about all the fun Craig was having with his dad.

Mary wished Jack would be a better dad to their kids but also wished he would just go away. While there were weekends they did not see their dad. The weekends they did see their dad were filled with turmoil and Jack's crazy mood swings and stories. While Brock took the brunt of the abuse, when Chris would stick up for Brock he would be punished too.

Angel was usually left out in the background being ignored. Angel was a shy, quiet little girl who often just sat and watched the craziness that went on around her. Mary would contact Child Protective

Services with concerns for her children's safety while

visiting with their father.   The social workers would

assure her that they were fine.   They

knew Lisa and had no reason to believe

there was anything to worry about.

Chapter Ten
Building Our Restart

Before long Lisa announced she was pregnant with Jack's baby.   Mark was sure now their time was over and Lisa had stepped over a line that they could never go back to the way things used to be.   Lisa would have weekends when they would have all five kids and she would ask other kids to spend the night too.   Lisa was trying to show everyone that she was the best mom around and people did not need to worry about her and Jack.

Lisa was convinced Jack was a great guy and people just had the wrong idea about him.   While Mary knew exactly how Jack was.   She had given up trying to prove he was dangerous.   All she could do was make the best of the time she had with her kids.   Mary knew there was safety in numbers but she also knew that so many kids were not easy to be around.   That was a lot of work.   Lisa continued to try and put up a front about her relationship with Jack but even if he had not been violent with Lisa, he was no help with the kids.   Lisa's kids or his own.   He had no desire to spend time with them or have them around.   That was all Lisa.

Mary was no longer interested in working with Lisa. While Lisa tried to force a relationship with Mary it was obvious that Lisa blamed Mary for Jack And Mary's break up.   Lisa believed Mary loved drinking more than her kids and Jack had no choice but to leave her.

No matter how much Mary told her they moved back to separate Lisa could not understand why Mary would not do everything in her power to keep Jack.   While Mary was happy to be rid of him.   She was just frustrated that her kids had to deal with him still.   Mary had resolved herself to the fact that there was not a lot she could do about it. She did know she did not want to work every day with Lisa.

Mary transferred to another county office. She was a good worker and it was not difficult for another opportunity to present itself for her. Mary was happy with her new job and while she did still have to hear things from the kids about what happened at Dad's house, she did not have to see Lisa everyday or work with her and that did make it easier. Even though it was a small town and most people knew everyone's business.

Lisa had a baby girl. They named her Beth. Lisa had hoped when Jack found out she was pregnant he would ask her to marry him. He did not. They were living together and that was enough for Jack. While Lisa did want to be married, she was willing to take what she could get to live with Jack. She had to convince herself she did not need a piece of paper to know their love was true. She knew Jack would come around and marry her one day. She just hoped it would be soon.

While Jack did nothing to deter Lisa from her daydreams of marrying him. Jack was not interested in getting married anytime soon. Jack resented how long it took him to get divorced from Mary and was not interested in going through another divorce. For now that was working for Lisa. Something about the way Jack talked. Women believed him and actually felt sorry for him. Lisa was willing to wait for as long as it took.

Now with Beth, Lisa had three kids and Mark was constantly questioning Lisa's parenting skills. Lisa was constantly having to defend herself to Mark. Mark had moved to another small town and had been hired on full time.   He had regular time off in which he

would have the kids.   Mark had met and married

another woman named Theresa.   He met her in the

new town when he moved.   They were very happy

together.   She had no children of her own but was

excited to participate in helping Mark with his children.

She loved the kids and worked hard to build a strong

relationship with both of them.   She wanted to be their

step-mom not their mom.   She was always very

careful to play the role she had and not overstep her

boundaries.   They were Mark's children.   She was

just helping him raise them while they were with them.

Lisa tried not to make waves with this new relationship

because she had tried so hard to be a good step-mom

to her own new family and wanted everyone to be

happy.   She knew some of the choices she had made

were not always the best but she had to live with those

choices and there was not a lot anyone could do about it.   She just tried to make the best of today.   Working hard to make her house a happy place to be.

Beth was a good baby and did not cause much disruption settling in.   Jack remained indifferent to the kids whether they were there or not he did what he wanted.   Jack was working but changing jobs was frequent for him.   Lisa was still working for the county and was most times their dependable income.   Jack was often doing his own thing and not worried about anyone else.   Lisa chose to let this be okay because she did not want to admit she may have made a mistake leaving Mark.

Mark was now working full time and they were working towards buying their own home in the new town he moved to.

Chapter Eleven
How Things Change

Not long after Beth was born Lisa found out she was

pregnant again.   This baby would be a boy.   Maybe

things would get better with Jack now that she was

having Jack's son.   Lisa could only hope.   They

would name the new baby boy Steven.

While Lisa had always had very easy pregnancies she

had a small scare with Beth and had several problems

carrying Steven.   Lisa had several doctor visits

resulting in an irregular heart beat being detected.

This had happened enough for her doctor to refer her

to a cardiologist.   Lisa had always been in good

health.   She had not had problems before but now

seemed to be having unexplained challenges with this

pregnancy.   Jack still could not be bothered.   He told

Lisa she was worried for nothing and everything would

be okay.

Lisa had always been a bit of a worrier about her health.   All she had to do was read or hear the symptoms and she would believe that she had whatever disease or illness it was listing the symptoms for.   Most people told her to stop reading or at least worrying about the symptoms.   Lisa couldn't help it.   She would convince herself she was sick. She had always gotten so concerned over symptoms she would go to the doctor and be told there was nothing wrong.   This time doctors were finding irregularities in the results.   But Lisa was choosing to believe Jack and tried not to worry about them.   Her family was growing and there was lots to do.

Mary was moving forward.   While she had not remarried she was dating and working hard to provide a good life for herself and her kids.   The kids were adjusting to their new life.   Their dad was busy making

a new life with Lisa but would take the kids to keep

Mary from having them.   Lisa would take on the

responsibility of caring for them while they were there.

Jack would come home every night but Lisa was

always the one who took care of the kids, all of them.

Steven was born with very little complications.   He

was a happy healthy baby boy.   Just eleven days after

Steven was born Lisa collapsed.   She was not

breathing and by the time the ambulance got there she

was dead.   Jack was working and they told him

something happened to Lisa.   By the time he got

to the hospital he was told Lisa was dead and they just

don't know why.   Her heart just stopped beating.

Now Jack was left with at least Beth and Steven full

time.

Lisa's parents were shocked at her sudden death and

decided to move in with Jack to help out with the kids. Jack had never done much to help out with any of the five kids he was father to. He welcomed the help from Lisa's parents.

It did not take long however, for Lisa's parents to become concerned by Jack's behavior and treatment of the kids. He was mean and quick to lose his temper. Beth and Steven were good kids but they were kids that needed a lot of attention right now with their mother taken away so quickly.

Steven was still a newborn and had not yet set a pattern of his routine. So it was difficult to get him into a comfortable pattern with so many changes. All Beth wanted was to be with adults. Always asking about her mother. It was hard to explain to such a little girl that her mom would no longer be around. Especially since everyone else was trying to deal with her sudden death as well.

Jack was frustrated having Lisa's parents in his house but knew he did not want to do this by himself. So he would need to try to keep his temper under control. Lisa's dad was suspicious of Jack and was having trouble believing that Lisa just all of a sudden would drop dead. He believed Jack had something to do with Lisa's death. He just did not know how. Mark was trying to work with Lisa's parents to see Beth and Steven because Craig and Connie had been with them as their sister and brother. Craig and Connie wanted to see them especially after they had lost their mom.

Lisa's parents tried to encourage that relationship but Jack was not interested. He told Lisa's parents there was really no need for them to continue to see Craig and Connie now that Lisa was gone. Mark did not agree. Mark was willing to go to court to make sure the kids got to see each other.   Jack would agree because he did not want to make trouble right now. He had enough to do.   Jack would allow visits with Craig and Connie for now.

As the weeks went by Lisa's dad got angrier and angrier with Jack.   Jack was not interested in the kids and was leaving Lisa's mom with the kids more and more.   While Jack would threaten almost daily to take the kids and move away with them.   Lisa's dad could take no more.   He convinced Jack to meet him in a secluded area and shot him in the head.   He wrapped him in an old carpet roll and drove him to the big city. He abandoned Jack's body in Lisa's mother's car and left the city.

Lisa's dad went back only to tell his wife what he had done and let her know he was going to run.   Lisa's mom did not want to run and was angry with him for what he had done.   Lisa's mom told him to go and she would try to send anyone asking questions away from him as best as she could.   It did not take long for word to get out that Jack had been found dead in Lisa's mom's car.

Lisa's mom was ready when the police came looking. She told them she did not know anything about it.   She told them her husband had taken the car last week and she had not seen him since.   She did not know what happened to Jack but that it was not unusual for him to be gone for days at a time.   While the police were not sure they believed it there was nothing more they could get out of Lisa's mom and she was taking care of the kids for now.

Lisa's mom did not know how long she would be taking care of the kids.   With the news of Jack's death his brother, Bill came back to the small town and demanded custody of Beth and Steven.   Jack's brother had no relationship with Beth or Steven.   Bill had not even met Lisa and Mark was not willing to let Beth and Steven go with Jack's brother, Bill.   If he could help it.

Mark would go to court and get custody of Beth and Steven.   He would raise them with their half brother and sister, Craig and Connie.   Mark was working full time, remarried and buying a house that was big enough for all of them.

Mary was shocked at the news of Jack's murder. Something changed inside her and all the horrible things Jack had done seemed to disappear.   Mary now idolized Jack and his life.   She changed her thinking about how he was because now he was gone and she could never get him back.   The kids would miss their dad but they had spent so much time without him it became an unattainable dream rather than an end to the violence.

It wasn't long after he started running that Lisa's dad turned himself in. He loved his wife and missed being with her but she would have nothing to do with him while he was on the run. She did not know that is what he was going to do and could not involve herself in something she had nothing to do with. Lisa's mom stayed with Krystal, Lisa's older sister and her new husband, Marcus. They had two boys together and welcomed her mom living with them. After Lisa's dad was sentenced to life in prison, Lisa's mom moved to the town by the prison so she could be close to him and visit as often as she could.

Krystal remained in the small town. She had a difficult time accepting Lisa's death. It seemed so hard to believe that life could change so fast and who would have guessed she would not live a long and wonderful life. Mary and Mark would get all the kids together often. It gave them all something to connect to with the death of Lisa. Lisa would have been so proud of all the kids she liked to call her own. Lisa always wanted nothing more than all of them to be together having a good time.

Connie and Beth looked just like Lisa and were a constant reminder of what they no longer had and of all that could have been with the loss of Lisa.

It was surprising but fantastic that Mark would turn out to be the one who kept Lisa's kids together. Never creating a separation that so many believed should be. Mark knew it was what would be best for his own kids, let alone for Beth and Steven.   He took on both of them as if they were his own and never looked back.

Mary met and married Jason. A man who had three

children.   They raised their six children in the small

town and continued being a part of Lisa's kids lives with

Mark.   It was the one thing the kids did have to hold on

to and made it easier for them to handle all that had

happened to them with the loss of Lisa

and Jack.

Families are who they are.   Regardless of what

judgments are made by others.   You cannot deny

family.   Everyone deserves to be happy with whoever

they call family and fill whatever time they have

together being happy.   Not fighting over things that in

the end do not really matter.

Chris, Brock, Angel,
Craig, Connie,
Beth and Steven

Be all you can be
Let no one choose your destiny.

ISBN 978-0-9890390-6-2